Panda Bear, Panda Bear, What Do You See?

By Bill Martin Jr
Pictures by Eric Carle

PUFFIN

Panda Bear,
Panda Bear,
what do you see?

A Note on Endangered Species

We are losing our animals. More than 5,000 animal species are endangered or threatened worldwide. This means that they are in danger of disappearing forever.

To safeguard these animals, there are over 3,500 protected areas in the form of parks, wildlife refuges and other reserves around the world. This book features ten of these endangered or threatened species.

We can all help save them by spreading the word about conservation.

The author wishes to thank Michael Sampson for his help in the preparation of this text.

PUFFIN BOOKS

Published by the Penguin Group
Penguin Books Ltd, 80 Strand, London WC2R 0RL, England
Penguin Putnam Inc., 375 Hudson Street, New York, New York 10014, USA
Penguin Books Australia Ltd, 250 Camberwell Road, Camberwell, Victoria 3124, Australia
Penguin Books Canada Ltd, 10 Alcorn Avenue, Toronto, Ontario, Canada M4V 3B2
Penguin Books India (P) Ltd, 11 Community Centre, Panchsheel Park, New Delhi – 110 017, India
Penguin Books (NZ) Ltd, Cnr Rosedale and Airborne Roads, Albany, Auckland, New Zealand
Penguin Books (South Africa) (Pty) Ltd, 24 Sturdee Avenue, Rosebank 2196, South Africa

Penguin Books Ltd, Registered Offices: 80 Strand, London WC2R 0RL, England

www.penguin.com

First published in the USA by Henry Holt and Company, LLC, 2003
Published in Great Britain in Puffin Books 2003
10 9 8 7 6 5 4 3 2 1

Text copyright © Bill Martin Jr, 2003
Illustrations copyright © Eric Carle, 2003

The moral right of the author and illustrator has been asserted

Manufactured in China

British Library Cataloguing in Publication Data
A CIP catalogue record for this book is available from the British Library

ISBN 0–141–38057–8

I see a bald eagle
soaring by me.

Bald Eagle,
Bald Eagle,
what do you see?

I see a water buffalo
charging by me.

Water Buffalo,
Water Buffalo,
what do you see?

I see a spider monkey
swinging by me.

Spider Monkey,
Spider Monkey,
what do you see?

I see a green sea turtle
swimming by me.

Green Sea Turtle,
Green Sea Turtle,
what do you see?

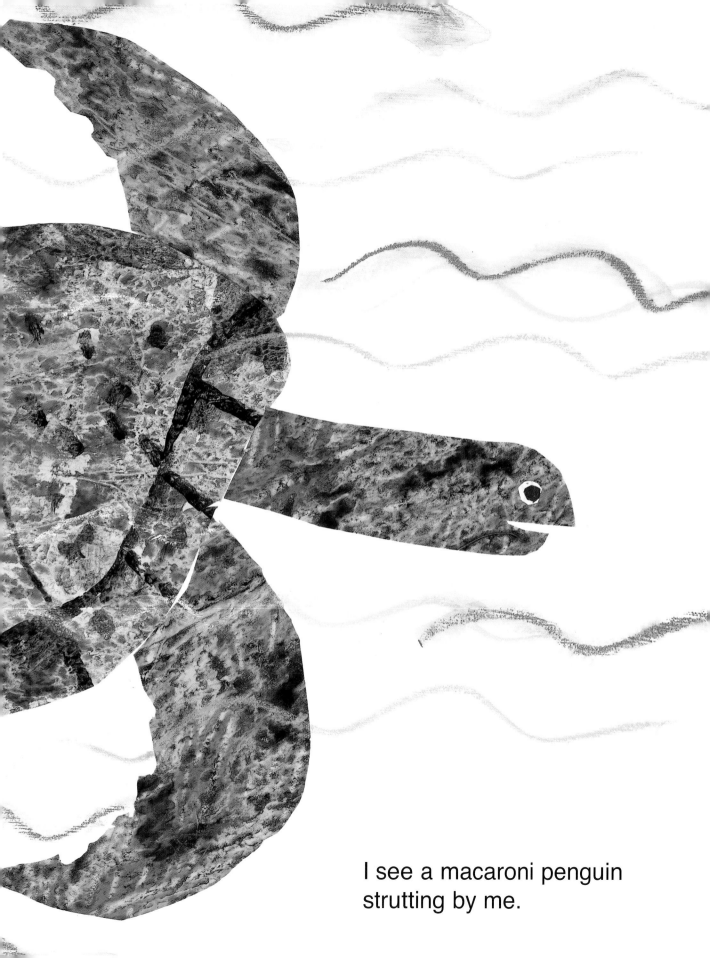

I see a macaroni penguin
strutting by me.

Macaroni Penguin,
Macaroni Penguin,
what do you see?

I see a sea lion
splashing by me.

Sea Lion,
Sea Lion,
what do you see?

I see a red wolf
sneaking by me.

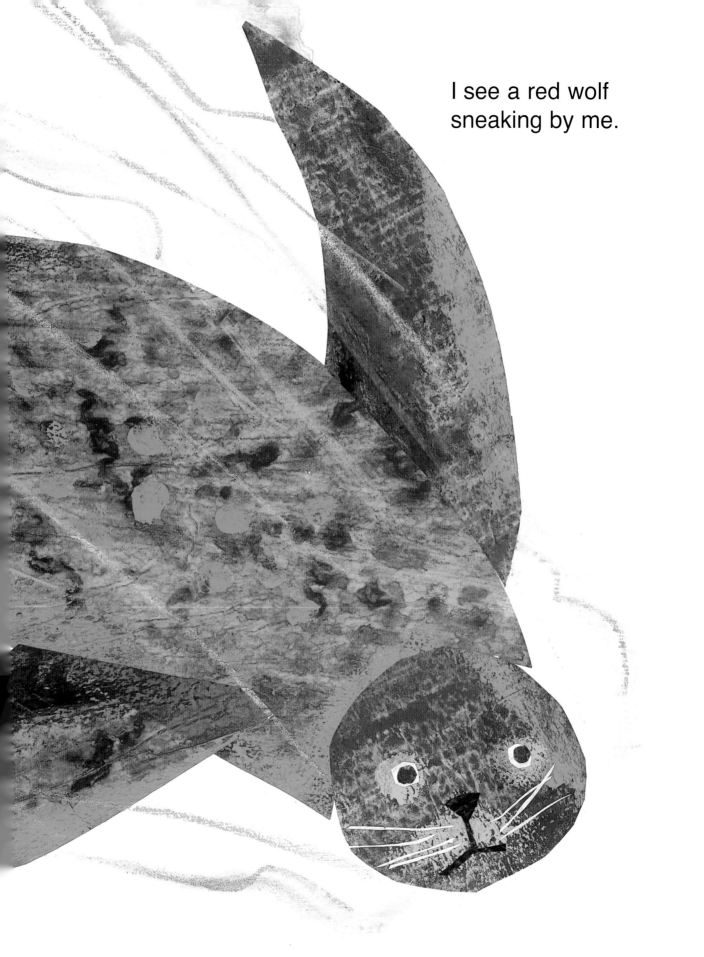

Red Wolf,
Red Wolf,
what do you see?

I see a whooping crane
flying by me.

Whooping Crane,
Whooping Crane,
what do you see?

I see a black panther
strolling by me.

Black Panther,
Black Panther,
what do you see?

I see a dreaming child
watching over me.

Dreaming Child,
Dreaming Child,
what do you see?

I see . . .

a panda bear,

a spider monkey,

a green sea turtle,

a red wolf,

a whooping crane,

a bald eagle,

a water buffalo,

a macaroni penguin,

a sea lion,

and a black panther . . .

**all wild and free –
that's what I see!**